Bears Make the Best
WRITING BUDDIES

written by
CARMEN OLIVER

illustrated by
JEAN CLAUDE

Raintree is an imprint of Capstone Global Library Limited, a company incorporated in England and Wales having its registered office at 264 Banbury Road, Oxford, OX2 7DY – Registered company number: 6695582

www.raintree.co.uk
myorders@raintree.co.uk

British Library Cataloguing in Publication Data
A full catalogue record for this book is available from the British Library.

ISBN: 978 1 4747 9306 3

For Bethany, who always gives a friend a hand and
is the best writing buddy a girl could ask for – C.O.

To João and Luís, all my love – J.C.

At writing time, Adelaide noticed Theo staring at his blank paper. He tapped his pencil. He fanned the pages. Then he pushed his notebook away with a giant sigh.

Adelaide wrote him a note and passed it along.

Relaxing in a quiet corner, Adelaide found Bear lost in a story.

"Come on," she coaxed. "There's someone who needs our help."

"Adelaide, what are you up to?" Mrs Fitz-Pea asked.

"Giving a friend a hand," said Adelaide. "Bears make the best writing buddies, and I'm going to tell Theo why."

"They know you never run away from a blank page. They encourage you to stay in your chair, and write the story only you can tell."

"If your ideas burrow and hibernate, Bear takes you fishing and foraging for new ones.

Before you know it, your beehive is buzzing and bursting with topics."

"Next, he reminds you to leave finger spaces as you drop word after word onto the page."

"Bears know that even the best writing buddies get frustrated sometimes, so stand up and stretch and ask, 'What happens next?'"

"And when you do, Bear delivers
a high-five and ROARRRS!"

"He asks you to share details you can see and smell. He asks for details you can hear, taste or touch."

"There's nothing you can't say when it comes from your heart. Because your voice is *your* voice - no two voices are the same."

"Whether your story is set in a village or a hot-air balloon, don't leave your main character hanging around with nothing to do."

"The sky's the limit, the possibilities are endless.

Keep building the action! Reeeeeach for the treetops.

And when your story can't go any further, claw and climb to the perfect ending."

Once there was a hot-air balloon

"Bears love a good cliffhanger, but they know when it's time to wrap it all up.

A first draft is just the start of good writing. The real magic begins when you rebuild, reimagine and rework."

REBUILD

REIMAGINE

AND REWORK

"And that is why bears make the very best writing buddies," Adelaide finished.

Theo snatched his pencil, opened his notebook and . . .

Bears are very big, and they like to eat honey.

. . . wrote page after page and never looked up – along with the rest of the class!

Adelaide wasn't surprised. She picked up her pencil and wrote in her notebook, "To be continued . . ."

Because her story needed a sequel starring . . .

. . . you guessed it – Bear.